# NORA'S ARK

# NORA'S ARK

By Natalie Kinsey-Warnock

*Illustrated by Emily Arnold McCully*

HARPERCOLLINSPUBLISHERS

When I was born, Grandma said I was so small I looked like a little bird. That's why I was named Wren. Grandma may look small, too, but she's made of granite, and she says I'm tough, just like she is. Good thing, or we never would have survived the 1927 Flood.

Grandma and Grandpa lived on a little farm by a river in Vermont. They didn't have much money, but there was always plenty to eat— milk from Grandpa's cows, vegetables from Grandma's garden, apples and plums from the orchard, fish from the river, and maple syrup that Grandpa and Grandma made each spring.

Grandpa was building Grandma a new house. It sat on a hill and, when finished, it would have electricity, a wringer washing machine, and best of all, an indoor bathroom.

"I don't need a new house, Horace," Grandma said. "We've lived here forty years, raised eight children, and been as happy as a family could be. That new house is just gravy."

"What do you mean?" I asked her.

Grandma thought how she could explain it to me.

"You like potatoes, don't you, Wren?"

"Yes, ma'am," I told her. Grandma made the best mashed potatoes in the world, with lots of milk, butter, and pepper in them. You could make a meal out of just her potatoes.

"You like gravy on them?"

"I reckon." Grandma did make good gravy. "But your potatoes taste good without gravy, too," I told her.

"Exactly," Grandma said. "Gravy tastes good, but you don't need it, and I don't need that new house. I like living here."

But Grandpa kept right on building.

When it began to rain on November 2, 1927, no one along the river had any idea nine inches of rain would fall in two days. Life in Vermont was about to change forever.

The rain came down in torrents. It drummed so loudly on the roof we couldn't talk. Grandma spent the morning baking bread. By noon, she'd made twenty-seven loaves.

"Grandma, why'd you make so much bread?" I shouted.

Grandma watched the water stream down the windows.

"We might need it," she said, but I couldn't imagine how we'd eat twenty-seven loaves of bread.

When Grandpa came in for lunch, he poured a quart of water out of each boot.

"I've never seen the river rise so fast," he said. "I think we'd best get up to the new house."

For once, Grandma didn't argue. By the time she'd packed quilts, candles, her photo albums, and a sack of potatoes, the water was up to the porch.

Grandpa let all the cows and horses out of the barn.

"What will happen to them?" I asked.

"They'll get to higher ground and be all right," he said. "Don't worry, Wren." But I could tell he was the one who was worried.

I loaded all those loaves of bread into my old baby carriage, covered it with an oilcloth, and pushed it through the mud and rain to the new house.

"Guess I built this place just in time," Grandpa said.

"If I didn't know better, I'd think you caused this flood just so I'd have to move into the new house," Grandma said, but she seemed glad to be on higher ground, too.

We'd scarcely set foot inside when we heard pounding on the door.

The three Guthrie boys stood on the porch, burlap bags in each hand. The bags squirmed and squawked.

"Our barn's flooded. Can we keep the chickens here?"

They emptied the chickens onto the kitchen floor.

"Some of our heifers are stranded in the fields," one of the boys said. "We're gonna see if we can push them to higher ground."

"I'll go with you," Grandpa said.

"May I go, too?" I asked.

"No!" Grandpa and Grandma both said at once.

"Be careful," Grandma told him, and he and the boys disappeared through the rain.

Even with all those chickens, the house seemed empty with Grandpa gone.

Grandma saw me shiver and wrapped a quilt around me.

"It's getting colder," she said. "I wish I had my cookstove here." She held me close as we stood watching the rain.

"I wish Grandpa would come back," I said.

"Me, too," said Grandma.

We both shrieked when a huge head appeared in the window. It was Major, one of the Fergusons' horses.

I was even more astonished when Grandma opened the door and led him in.

"You're bringing Major into the house?"

"We don't have a stove," Grandma said. "He's big. He'll add heat to the place."

Major took up half the kitchen. The other half was taken up by loaves of bread and chickens.

We had chickens in the cupboards, chickens on the shelves and in the baby carriage, even chickens roosting on Major's back.

Our next visitors were Mrs. Lafleur and her daughter, Madeleine. Mrs. Lafleur didn't speak much English.

"Our house wash away," Mrs. Lafleur said. "We row boat here."

Madeleine looked around the kitchen, and her eyes opened wide.

"Des poulets dans le chariot de bébé?" she said. I guess she'd never seen chickens in a baby carriage before.

By nightfall, the house was full to bursting. Besides Mrs. Lafleur
and Madeleine, Mr. and Mrs. Guthrie, the Fergusons, and the Craig

family had moved in, twenty-three people in all. There were also three
horses, a cow, five pigs, a duck, four cats, and one hundred chickens.

The river rose until the house became an island, and we
watched our neighbors' houses wash down the river.

Mr. and Mrs. Guthrie had brought a side of salt pork with them, though we had no way to cook it. The Fergusons had saved their radio, a skillet, a bag of dried apples, and a three-legged cat. They were delighted to find Major alive and well and in our kitchen.

The Craigs had lost everything but the clothes on their backs.

"We're just glad we all got out alive," Mrs. Craig said, which only reminded Grandma and me that Grandpa had still not returned.

We had bread and dried apples for supper, and rainwater Madeleine and I scooped out of the Lafleurs' rowboat. The water had a few fish scales in it, but no one complained.

With no stove or beds, we all huddled together for warmth, sharing Grandma's quilts as best we could. We sang Scottish songs and "Row, Row, Row Your Boat" in a round, and Mrs. Lafleur taught us "À la Claire Fontaine," a tune that brought tears to our eyes even though we couldn't understand the words. Mrs. Guthrie told how her grandfather had fought at Gettysburg, and Mr. Craig kept us laughing with stories of his boyhood days in a logging camp in Maine. If it hadn't been for the thought of Grandpa out there somewhere, it would have almost seemed like a party.

I knew Grandma was worried about Grandpa. I was worried, too. He should have been home by now.

I wanted to ask Peter Ferguson if he would come with me to look for Grandpa, but I knew if Grandma overheard she'd forbid me to go, so when the sky was getting light, I sneaked out and sprinted for the rowboat.

Grandma was just getting into it.

"What are you doing here?" she wanted to know.

"Same as you, I reckon. Going to look for Grandpa."

"It's too dangerous," Grandma said. "Go back to the house," but I shook my head.

Grandma looked at me hard.

"All right," she said. "We'll look for him together."

I pushed us off into water that was full of furniture and trees and dead animals. Grandma had to be careful where she rowed. It was raining so hard I had to keep bailing water out of the boat.

Nothing looked the same. Fields had become lakes. Just the
roofs of houses stuck up above the water.

On one of those roofs we saw a dog.

"Why, I believe that's Sam Burroughs' collie," Grandma said,
and she rowed toward the house. The collie barked when she saw
us coming.

I held on to the roof to steady the boat.

"Come on, girl," I said, and the dog jumped into the boat beside me. She whined and licked my face.

The strangest sight was yet to come. We rounded a bend in the river and I squinted, sure that my eyes were fooling me. Then I heard Grandma's voice behind me.

"Wren, are these old eyes failing me, or is that a cow in a tree?" Grandma asked.

It was indeed. A red and white Ayrshire was wedged into the crook formed by two branches, and she was bawling piteously. Higher up in the branches was a man. He was hollering almost as loudly as the cow.

"I believe we've found your grandpa," Grandma said, relief flooding her face.

"I was on my way home when I got swept away by the water," Grandpa said. "I thought I was a goner, too, but when this cow floated by, I grabbed her tail and stayed afloat until she got hung up in this tree."

We pushed and pulled on that cow, but she was stuck fast and we finally had to leave her. Grandpa promised he'd come back and try to cut her free, but he was crying as we rowed away.

"Goodness," Grandma said. "All that fuss over a cow." But Grandpa wasn't crying over just one cow.

"All our cows drowned, Nora," he said. "The house, the barn, the horses, they're all gone."

Grandma wiped the tears from his cheeks.

"You're safe, and that's all that matters," she said.

"We'll have to start over," Grandpa said, and Grandma smiled.

"We can do that," she said.

Grandpa smiled back at her, and I knew then that, no matter what, everything would be all right.

The Craigs, Fergusons, Guthries, and Lafleurs were glad to see us. Madeleine even hugged me.

"She was afraid you'd drowned," Peter said. He blushed. "I was, too," he added.

When Grandpa saw all the animals in the kitchen, he burst out laughing.

"Nora, I thought I was building you a house, but I see it was really an ark."

It took three days for the water to go down enough so our neighbors could go see what was left of their farms.

Grandpa put his arm around Grandma.

"I'll finish this house the way you want it, Nora," he said. But he shook his head when the Fergusons led Major out.

"I don't know as I'll ever be able to get those hoofprints out of this floor," he said.

I've now lived in my grandparents' house for more than forty years, and those hoofprints are still in the floor. I never sanded them out because they remind me of what's important: family and friends and neighbors helping neighbors.

Like Grandma said, everything else is just gravy.

# AUTHOR'S NOTE

The Flood of 1927 was the worst disaster in Vermont's history. Eighty-four people died, including the state's lieutenant governor, and nine thousand people were driven from their homes. Two thousand cows drowned, and more than seven thousand acres of farmland were washed away or covered by flood debris. The flood destroyed 1,450 bridges and hundreds of miles of railroad tracks and dirt roads.

As in all disasters, there were stories of courage and compassion and of people helping one another. This is one of those stories.

To family, friends, and good neighbors who have helped
my family weather a storm
—N.K.-W.


For Harriet and Jim
—E.A.M.

Nora's Ark
Text copyright © 2005 by Natalie Kinsey-Warnock
Illustrations copyright © 2005 by Emily Arnold McCully
Manufactured in China by South China Printing Company Ltd. All rights reserved. No part of this book may be used or reproduced in any manner whatsoever without written permission except in the case of brief quotations embodied in critical articles and reviews. For information address HarperCollins Children's Books, a division of HarperCollins Publishers, 1350 Avenue of the Americas, New York, NY 10019.
www.harperchildrens.com
Library of Congress Cataloging-in-Publication Data
Kinsey-Warnock, Natalie.
Nora's Ark / by Natalie Kinsey-Warnock ; illustrated by Emily Arnold McCully.—1st ed.
p.    cm.
Summary: During the Vermont flood of 1927, a girl and her grandparents share their new hilltop house with neighbors and animals.
ISBN 0-688-17244-X — ISBN 0-06-029517-1 (lib. bdg.)
[1. Floods—Fiction.   2. Vermont—History—20th century—Fiction.   3. Farm life—Vermont—Fiction.
4. Grandparents—Fiction.]   I. McCully, Emily Arnold, ill.   II. Title.
PZ7.K6293No   2005
[E]—dc22
2004003444
Typography by Al Cetta        3  4  5  6  7  8  9  10    ❖    First Edition